FOR
SEBASTIAN
WALKER
C.V.

ELSIE
PIDDOCK
SKIPS IN HER SLEEP

ELEANOR FARJEON

illustrated by
CHARLOTTE VOAKE

CANDLEWICK PRESS

Elsie Piddock lived in Glynde under Caburn, where lots of other little girls lived too. They lived mostly on bread-and-butter, because their mothers were too poor to buy cake. As soon as Elsie began to hear, she heard the other little girls skipping every evening after school in the lane outside her mother's cottage. *Swish-swish!* went the rope through the air. *Tappity-tap!* went the little girls' feet on the ground. *Mumble-umble-umble!* went the children's voices, saying a rhyme that the skipper could skip to.

In course of time, Elsie not only heard the sounds, but understood what they were all about, and then the mumble-umble turned itself into words like this:

ANdy SPANdy SUGARdy CANdy,
FRENCH ALmond ROCK!
Breadandbutterforyoursupper's
allyourmother's
GOT!

The second bit went twice as fast as the first bit, and when the little girls said it Elsie Piddock, munching her supper, always munched her mouthful of bread-and-butter in double-quick time. She wished she had some Sugardy-Candy-French-Almond-Rock to suck during the first bit, but she never had.

When Elsie Piddock was three years old, she asked her mother for a skipping-rope.

"You're too little," said her mother. "Bide a bit till you're a bigger girl, then you shall have one."

Elsie pouted, and said no more. But in the middle of the night her parents were wakened by something going *Slap-slap!* on the floor, and there was Elsie in her nightgown skipping with her father's braces.

She skipped till her feet caught in the tail of them, and she tumbled down and cried. But she had skipped ten times running first.

"Bless my buttons, mother!" said Mr. Piddock. "The child's a born skipper."

And Mrs. Piddock jumped out of bed full of pride, rubbed Elsie's elbows for her, and said: "There-a-there now! Dry your tears, and tomorrow you shall have a skip-rope all of your own."

So Elsie dried her eyes on the hem of her nightgown; and in the morning, before he went to work, Mr. Piddock got a little cord, just the right length, and made two little wooden handles to go on the ends.

With this Elsie skipped all day, scarcely stopping to eat her breakfast of bread-and-butter, and her dinner of butter-and-bread.

And in the evening, when the school-children were gathered in the lane, Elsie went out among them, and began to skip with the best.

"Oh!" cried Joan Challon, who was the champion skipper of them all, "just look at little Elsie Piddock skipping as never so!"

All the skippers stopped to look, and then to wonder. Elsie Piddock certainly *did* skip as never so, and they called to their mothers to come and see. And the mothers in the lane came to their doors, and threw up their hands, and cried: "Little Elsie Piddock is a born skipper!"

By the time she was
five she could outskip
any of them: whether
in "Andy-Spandy," "Lady, Lady, Drop your
Purse," "Charley Parley Stole some Barley,"
or whichever of the games it might be.

By the time she was six her name and fame were known to all the villages in the county. And by the time she was seven, the fairies heard of her.

They were fond of skipping
themselves, and they had a
special Skipping-Master who
taught them new skips every
month at the new moon.
As they skipped they
chanted:

The High Skip,

The Sly Skip,

The Skip Like a Feather,

The Long Skip,

The Strong Skip,

And the Skip All Together!

The Slow Skip,

The Toe Skip,

The Skip Double-Double,

The Fast Skip,

The Last Skip,

And the Skip Against Trouble!

All these skips had their own meanings, and were made up by the Skipping-Master, whose name was Andy-Spandy. He was very proud of his fairies, because they skipped better than the fairies of any other county; but he was also very severe with them if they did not please him.

One night he scolded Fairy Heels-o'-Lead for skipping badly, and praised Fairy Flea-Foot for skipping well. Then Fairy Heels-o'-Lead sniffed and snuffed, and said: "Hhm-hhm-hhm! There's a little girl in Glynde who could skip Flea-Foot round the moon and back again. A born skipper she is, and she skips as never so."

"What is her name?" asked Andy-Spandy.

"Her name is Elsie Piddock, and she has

skipped down every village far and near, from Didling to Wannock."

"Go and fetch her here!" commanded Andy-Spandy.

Off went Heels-o'-Lead, and poked her head through Elsie's little window under the eaves, crying: "Elsie Piddock! Elsie Piddock! there's a Skipping Match on Caburn, and Fairy Flea-Foot says she can skip better than you."

Elsie Piddock was fast asleep, but the words got into her dream, so she hopped out of bed with her eyes closed, took her skipping-rope,

and followed Heels-o'-Lead to the top of
Mount Caburn, where Andy-Spandy and
the fairies were waiting for them.

"Skip, Elsie Piddock!" said Andy-Spandy,
"and show us what you're worth!"

Elsie twirled her rope and skipped in her
sleep, and as she skipped she murmured:

ANdy SPANdy SUGARdy CANdy,

FRENCH ALmond ROCK!

Breadandbutterforyoursupper's

allyourmother's

GOT!

Andy-Spandy watched her skipping with his eyes as sharp as needles, but he could find no fault with it, nor could the fairies.

"Very good, as far as it goes!" said Andy-Spandy. "Now let us see how far it *does* go. Stand forth, Elsie and Flea-Foot, for the Long Skip."

Elsie had never done the Long Skip, and if she had had all her wits about her she wouldn't have known what Andy-Spandy meant; but as she was dreaming, she

understood him perfectly. So she twirled
her rope, and as it came over jumped as far
along the ground as she could, about twelve
feet from where she had started. Then
Flea-Foot did the Long Skip, and skipped
clean out of sight.

"Hum!" said Andy-Spandy. "Now, Elsie
Piddock, let us see you do the Strong Skip."

Once more Elsie understood what was
wanted of her; she put both feet together,
jumped her rope, and came down with all
her strength, so that her heels sank into the
ground. Then Flea-Foot did the Strong Skip,

and sank into the ground as deep as her
waist.

"Hum!" said Andy-Spandy. "And now,
Elsie Piddock, let us see you do the Skip All
Together."

At his words, all the fairies leaped to
their ropes, and began skipping as lively as
they could, and Elsie with them. An hour
went by, two hours, and three hours; one
by one the fairies fell down exhausted,
and Elsie Piddock skipped on. Just before
morning she was skipping all by herself.

Then Andy-Spandy wagged his head
and said: "Elsie Piddock, you are a born
skipper. There's no tiring you at all. And
for that you shall come once a month to
Caburn when the moon is new, and I will
teach you to skip till a year is up. And after
that I'll wager there won't be mortal or fairy
to touch you."

Andy-Spandy was as good as his word.
Twelve times during the next year Elsie
Piddock rose up in her sleep with the new

moon, and went to the top of Mount Caburn. There she took her place among the fairies, and learned to do all the tricks of the skipping-rope, until she did them better than any. At the end of the year she did the High Skip so well, that she skipped right over the moon.

In the Sly Skip not a fairy could catch her, or know where she would skip to next; so artful was she, that she could skip through the lattice of a skeleton leaf, and never break it.

She redoubled the Skip
Double-Double, in which you
only had to double yourself up
twice round the skipping-rope
before it came down. Elsie Piddock
did it four times.

In the Fast Skip, she skipped so fast that
you couldn't see her, though she stood on
the same spot all the time.

In the Last Skip, when all the fairies skipped over the same rope in turn, running round and round till they made a mistake from giddiness, Elsie never got giddy, and never made a mistake, and was always left in last.

In the Slow Skip, she skipped so slow that a mole had time to throw up his hill

under her rope before
she came down.

In the Toe Skip,
when all the others
skipped on their
tip-toes, Elsie never
touched a grass-blade

with more than the edge of her toe-nail.

In the Skip Against Trouble, she skipped
so joyously that Andy-Spandy himself
chuckled with delight.

In the Long Skip she skipped from
Caburn to the other end of Sussex, and had
to be fetched back by the wind.

In the Strong Skip, she went right under
the earth, as a diver goes under the sea,
and the rabbits, whose burrows she had

disturbed, handed her
up again.

But in the Skip Like
a Feather she came
down like gossamer,
so that she could alight
on a spider-thread
and never shake the
dew-drop off.

And in the Skip
All Together, she could skip
down the whole tribe of fairies,
and remain as fresh as a daisy. Nobody had
ever found out how long Elsie Piddock could
skip without getting tired, for everybody
else got tired first. Even Andy-Spandy
didn't know.

At the end of the year he said to her: "Elsie Piddock, I have taught you all. Bring me your skipping-rope, and you shall have a prize."

Elsie gave her rope to Andy-Spandy, and he licked the two little wooden handles, first the one and then the other. When he

handed the rope back to her, one of the handles was made of Sugar Candy, and the other of French Almond Rock.

"There!" said Andy-Spandy. "Though you suck them never so, they will never grow less, and you shall therefore suck sweet all your life. And as long as you are little enough to skip with this rope, you shall skip as I have taught you. But when you are too big for this rope, and must get a new one, you will no longer be able to do all the fairy skips that you have learned, although you will still skip better in the mortal way than any other girl that ever was born. Good-bye, Elsie Piddock."

"Aren't I ever going to skip for you again?" asked Elsie Piddock in her sleep.

But Andy-Spandy didn't answer. For morning had come over the Downs, and the fairies disappeared, and Elsie Piddock went back to bed.

If Elsie had been famous for her skipping before this fairy year, you can imagine what she became after it. She created so much wonder, that she hardly dared to show all she could do.

Nevertheless, for another year she did such incredible things, that people came from far and near to see her skip over the church spire, or through the split oak-tree in the Lord's Park, or across the river at its widest point.

When there was trouble in her mother's house, or in any house in the village, Elsie

Piddock skipped so gaily that the trouble was forgotten in laughter.

And when she skipped all the old games in Glynde, along with the little girls, and they sang:

ANdy SPANdy SUGARdy CANdy,
FRENCH ALmond ROCK!
Breadandbutterforyoursupper's
allyourmother's
GOT!

Elsie Piddock said: "It aren't all *I've* got!"
and gave them a suck of her skipping-
rope handles all round.

And on the night of
the new moon, she always
led the children up Mount Caburn,
where she skipped more marvellously
than ever.

In fact, it was Elsie Piddock who
established the custom of New-Moon-
Skipping on Caburn.

But at the end of another year she had
grown too big to skip with her little rope.
She laid it away in a box, and went on
skipping with a longer one. She still skipped
as never so, but her fairy tricks were laid
by with the rope, and though her friends
teased her to do the marvellous things she
used to do, Elsie Piddock only laughed,
and shook her head, and never told why.
In time, when she was still the pride and
wonder of her village, people would say:
"Ah, but you should ha' seen her when she
was a littling! Why, she could skip through
her mother's keyhole!" And in more time,
these stories became a legend that nobody
believed. And in still more time, Elsie grew
up (though never very much), and became a

little woman, and gave up skipping, because skipping-time was over. After fifty years or so, nobody remembered that she had ever skipped at all. Only Elsie knew. For when times were hard, and they often were, she sat by the hearth with her dry crust and no butter, and sucked the Sugar Candy that Andy-Spandy had given her for life.

It was ever and ever so long afterwards. Three new Lords had walked in the Park since the day when Elsie Piddock had skipped through the split oak. Changes had come in the village; old families

had died out, new families had arrived;
others had moved away to distant parts,
the Piddocks among them. Farms had
changed hands, cottages had been pulled
down, and new ones had been built.

But Mount Caburn was as it always had
been, and as the people came to think it
always would be. And still the children kept
the custom of going there each new moon
to skip. Nobody remembered how this
custom had come about, it was too far back
in the years. But customs are customs, and
the child who could not skip the new moon
in on Caburn stayed at home and cried.

Then a new Lord came to the Park;
one not born a Lord, who had grown rich
in trade, and bought the old estate. Soon
after his coming, changes began to take
place more violent than the pulling down
of cottages. The new Lord began to shut
up footpaths and destroy rights of way. He
stole the Common rights here and there, as

he could. In his greed for more than he had
got, he raised rents and pressed the people
harder than they could bear. But bad as the
high rents were to them, they did not mind
these so much as the loss of their old rights.
They fought the new Lord, trying to keep
what had been theirs for centuries, and
sometimes they won the fight, but oftener
lost it. The constant quarrels bred a spirit of

anger between them and the Lord, and out of hate he was prepared to do whatever he could to spite them.

Amongst the lands over which he exercised a certain power was Caburn. This had been always open to the people, and the Lord determined if he could to close it. Looking up the old deeds, he discovered that, though the Down was his, he was obliged to leave a way upon it by which the people could go from one village to another. For hundreds of years they had made a short cut of it over the top.

The Lord's Lawyer told him that, by the wording of the deeds, he could never stop the people from travelling by way of the Downs.

"Can't I!" snorted the Lord. "Then at least I will make them travel a long way round!"

And he had plans drawn up to enclose the whole of the top of Caburn, so that nobody could walk on it. This meant that the people must trudge miles round the base, as they passed from place to place.

The Lord gave out that he needed Mount Caburn to build great factories on.

The village was up in arms to defend its rights.

"Can he do it?" they asked those who knew; and they were told: "It is not quite certain, but we fear he can." The Lord himself was not quite certain either but he went on with his plans, and each new move was watched with anger and anxiety by the villagers. And not only by the villagers;  for the fairies saw that their own skipping-ground was threatened. How could they ever skip there again when the grass was turned to cinders, and the new moon blackened by chimney-smoke?

The Lawyer said to the Lord: "The people will fight you tooth and nail."

"Let 'em!" blustered the Lord; and he asked uneasily: "Have they a leg to stand on?"

"Just half a leg," said the Lawyer. "It would be as well not to begin building yet, and if you can come to terms with them you'd better."

The Lord sent word to the villagers that, though he undoubtedly could do what he pleased, he would, out of his good heart, restore to them a footpath he had blocked, if they would give up all pretensions to Caburn.

"Footpath, indeed!" cried stout John Maltman, among his cronies at the Inn. "What's a footpath to Caburn? Why, our mothers skipped there as children, and our children skip there now. And we hope to see our children's children skip there. If Caburn top be built over, 'twill fair break my little Ellen's heart."

"Ay, and my Margery's," said another.

"And my Mary's and Kitty's!" cried a third. Others spoke up, for nearly all had daughters whose joy it was to skip on Caburn at the new moon.

John Maltman turned to their best adviser, who had studied the matter closely, and asked: "What think ye? Have we a leg to stand on?"

"Only half a one," said the other. "I doubt if you can stop him. It might be as well to come to terms."

"None of his footpaths for us," swore stout John Maltman. "We'll fight the matter out."

So things were left for a little, and each side wondered what the next move would be. Only the people knew in their hearts that they must be beaten in the end and the Lord was sure of his victory. So sure, that he had great loads of bricks ordered; but he did not begin building for fear the people might grow violent, and perhaps burn his ricks and destroy his property.

The only thing he did was to put a wire fence round the top of Caburn, and set a

keeper there to send the people round it.
The people broke the fence in many places,
and jumped it, and crawled

under it; and as the keeper could not be
everywhere at once, many of them crossed
the Down almost under his nose.

KEEP
OUT

One evening, just before the new moon was due, Ellen Maltman went into the woods to cry. For she was the best skipper under Mount Caburn, and the thought that she would never skip there again made her more unhappy than she had ever

thought she could
be. While she was
crying in the dark,
she felt a hand on her
shoulder, and a voice
said to her: "Crying for
trouble, my dear? That'll
never do!"

The voice might have been the voice of a withered leaf, it was so light and dry; but it was also kind, so Ellen checked her sobs and said: "It's a big trouble, ma'am, there's no remedy against it *but* to cry."

"Why, yes, there is," said the withered voice. "Ye should skip against trouble, my dear."

At this Ellen's sobs burst forth anew. "I'll never skip no more!" she wailed. "If I can't skip the new moon in on Caburn, I'll never skip no more."

"And why can't you skip the new moon in on Caburn?" asked the voice.

Then Ellen told her.

After a little pause the voice spoke quietly out of the darkness. "It's more than you will break their hearts if they cannot skip on Caburn. And it must not be, it must not be. Tell me your name."

"Ellen Maltman, ma'am, and I do love skipping. I can skip down anybody, ma'am, and they say I skip as never so!"

"They do, do they?" said the withered voice. "Well, Ellen, run you home and tell them this. They are to go to this Lord and tell him he shall have his way and build on Caburn, if he will first take down the fence and let all who have ever skipped there skip there once more by turns, at the new moon. *All,* mind you, Ellen. And when the last skipper skips the last skip, he may lay his first brick. And let it be written out on paper, and signed and sealed."

"But ma'am!" said Ellen, wondering.

"No words, child. Do as I tell you." And

the withered voice sounded so compelling that Ellen resisted no more. She ran straight to the village, and told her story to everybody.

At first they could hardly swallow it; and even when they had swallowed it, they said: "But what's the sense of it?" But Ellen persisted and persisted; something of the spirit of the old voice got into her words, and against their reason the people began to think it was the thing to do. To cut a long story

short they sent the message to the Lord
next day.

The Lord could scarcely believe his ears.
He rubbed his hands, and chortled at the
people for fools.

"They've come to terms!" he sneered.
"I shall have the Down, and keep my
footpath too. Well, they shall have their
Skipping-Party; and the moment it is ended,
up go my factories!"

The paper was
drawn out, signed
by both parties
in the presence
of witnesses,
and duly
sealed; and

on the night of the new moon, the Lord
invited a party of his friends to go with
him to Caburn to see the sight.

And what a sight it was for them to
see; every little girl in the village was there
with her skipping-rope, from the toddlers
to those who had just turned up their hair.
Nay, even the grown maidens and the
young mothers were there; and the very
matrons too had come with ropes. Had not
they once as children skipped on Caburn?
And the message had said "All."

Yes, and others were there, others they could not see: Andy-Spandy and his fairy team, Heels-o'-Lead, Flea-Foot, and all of the rest, were gathered round to watch with bright fierce eyes the last great skipping on their precious ground.

The skipping began. The
toddlers first, a skip
or so apiece, a
stumble, and
they fell out.
The Lord
and his party
laughed aloud at
the comical mites, and at another time
the villagers would have laughed too.
But there was no laughter in
them tonight. Their eyes
were bright and fierce like
those of the fairies. After
the toddlers the little girls
skipped in the order of their ages, and
as they got older, the skipping got better.

In the thick of the schoolchildren, "This will take some time," said the Lord impatiently. And when Ellen Maltman's turn came, and she went into her thousands, he grew restive. But even she, who could skip as never so, tired at last; her foot tripped, and she fell on the ground with a little sob. None lasted even half her time; of those who followed some were better, some were worse, than others; and in the small hours the older women were beginning to take their turn. Few of them kept it up for half a minute; they hopped and puffed bravely,

but their skipping days were done. As
they had laughed at the babies, so now the
Lord's friends jibed at the babies'
grandmothers.

"Soon over now," said the
Lord, as the oldest of the women
who had come to skip, a fat old
dame of sixty-seven, stepped
out and twirled her rope.

Her foot
caught in it; she staggered,
dropped the rope, and hid
her face in her hands.

"Done!" shouted the
Lord; and he brandished at
the crowd a trowel and a
brick which he had brought with

him. "Clear out, the lot of you! I am going to lay the first brick. The skipping's ended!"

"No, if you please," said a gentle withered voice, "it is *my* turn now." And out of the crowd stepped a tiny tiny woman, so very old, so very bent and fragile, that she seemed to be no bigger than a little child.

"You!" cried the Lord. "Who are *you*?"

"My name is Elsie Piddock, if you please, and I am a hundred and nine years old. For the last seventy-nine years I have lived over the border, but I was born in Glynde, and I skipped on Caburn as a child." She spoke like one in a dream, and her eyes were closed.

"Elsie Piddock! Elsie Piddock!" the name ran in a whisper round the crowd.

"Elsie Piddock!" murmured Ellen Maltman. "Why, Mum, I thought Elsie Piddock was just a tale."

"Nay, Elsie Piddock was no tale!" said the fat woman who had skipped last. "My mother Joan skipped with her many a time, and told me tales you never would believe."

"Elsie Piddock!" they all breathed again; and a wind seemed to fly round Mount Caburn, shrilling the name with glee. But it was no wind, it was Andy-Spandy and his fairy team, for they had seen the skipping-rope in the tiny woman's hands. One of the

handles was made of Sugar Candy, and the other was made of French Almond Rock.

But the new Lord had never even heard of Elsie Piddock as a story; so laughing coarsely once again, he said: "One more bump for an old woman's bones! Skip, Elsie Piddock, and show us what you're worth."

"Yes, skip, Elsie Piddock," cried Andy-Spandy and the fairies, "and show them what you're worth!"

Then Elsie Piddock stepped into the middle of the onlookers, twirled her baby rope over her little shrunken body, and began to skip. And she skipped as NEVER so!

First of all she skipped:

ANdy SPANdy SUGARdy CANdy,
FRENCH ALmond ROCK!
Breadandbutterforyoursupper's
allyourmother's
GOT!

And nobody could find fault with her
skipping. Even the Lord gasped: "Wonderful!
wonderful for an old woman!" But Ellen
Maltman, who *knew,*
whispered: "Oh, Mum!
'tis wonderful for
*any*body! And oh Mum,
do but see—she's skipping
in her sleep!"

It was true. Elsie Piddock, shrunk to the size of seven years old, was sound asleep, skipping the new moon in with her baby rope that was up to all the tricks. An hour went by, two hours, three hours. There was no stopping her, and no tiring her. The people gasped, the Lord fumed, and the fairies turned head-over-heels for joy. When morning broke the Lord cried: "That's enough!"

But Elsie Piddock went on skipping.

"Time's up!" cried the Lord.

"When I skip my last skip, you shall lay your first brick," said Elsie Piddock.

The villagers broke into a cheer.

"Signed and sealed, my Lord, signed and sealed," said Elsie Piddock.

"But hang it, old

woman, you

can't go on for ever!" cried the Lord.

"Oh yes, I can," said Elsie Piddock. And on she went.

At midday the Lord shouted: "Will the woman never stop?"

"No, she won't," said Elsie Piddock. And she didn't.

"Then I'll stop you!" stormed
the Lord, and made a grab at her.

"Now for a Sly Skip," said Elsie
Piddock, and skipped right through
his thumb and forefinger.

"Hold her, you!" yelled the Lord
to his Lawyer.

"Now for a High Skip," said
Elsie Piddock, and as the
Lawyer darted at her,
she skipped right
over the highest
lark singing in
the sun.

The villagers
shouted for glee,
and the Lord and
his friends were furious.
Forgotten was the compact signed and
sealed—their one thought now was to seize
the maddening old woman, and stop her
skipping by sheer force.

But they couldn't. She played all her tricks on them:

High Skip,

Slow Skip,

Sly Skip,

Toe Skip,

Long Skip,

Fast Skip,

Strong Skip,

but never Last Skip.

On and on and on she went.

When the sun began to set, she was still skipping.

"Can we never rid the Down of the old thing?" cried the Lord desperately.

"No," answered Elsie Piddock in her sleep, "the Down will never be rid of me more. It's the children of Glynde I'm skipping for, to hold the Down for them

and theirs for ever; it's Andy-Spandy I'm
skipping for once again, for through him I've
sucked sweet all my life. Oh, Andy, even
you never knew how long Elsie Piddock
could go on skipping!"

"The woman's mad!" cried the Lord.
"Signed and sealed doesn't hold with a
madwoman. Skip or no skip, I shall lay the
first brick!"

He plunged his trowel into the ground,
and forced his brick
down into the hole as
a token of his possession
of the land.

"Now," said Elsie
Piddock, "for a Strong Skip!"

Right on the top of the brick she

skipped, and down underground she sank
out of sight, bearing the brick beneath her.
Wild with rage, the Lord dived after her.

Up came Elsie Piddock skipping blither than ever—but the Lord never came up again. The Lawyer ran to look down the hole; but there was no sign of him. The Lawyer reached his arm down the hole; but there was no reaching him. The Lawyer dropped a pebble down the hole; and no one heard it fall. So strong had Elsie Piddock skipped the Strong Skip.

The Lawyer shrugged his shoulders, and
he and the Lord's friends left Mount Caburn
for good and all. Oh, how joyously Elsie
Piddock skipped then!

"Skip Against Trouble!" cried she, and
skipped so that everyone present burst into
happy laughter. To the tune of it she skipped
the Long Skip, clean out of sight.

And the people went home to tea.
Caburn was saved for their children,
and for the fairies, for ever.

But that wasn't the end of Elsie Piddock; she has never stopped skipping on Caburn since, for Signed and Sealed is Signed and Sealed. Not many have seen her, because she knows all the tricks; but if you go to Caburn at the new moon, you may catch a glimpse of a tiny bent figure, no bigger than a child, skipping all by itself in its sleep, and hear a gay little voice, like the voice of a dancing yellow leaf, singing:

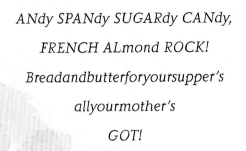

ANdy SPANdy SUGARdy CANdy,

FRENCH ALmond ROCK!

Breadandbutterforyoursupper's

allyourmother's

GOT!

"The high skip,
the sly skip,
the skip like a feather,
the long skip,
the strong skip,
and the skip all together!
The slow skip,
the toe skip,
the skip double-double,
the fast skip,
the last skip,
and the skip against
trouble!"

Eleanor Farjeon (1881–1965) was one of the most important children's writers of the twentieth century. A fine poet, she also wrote many stories for the young. She had no formal education and spent her childhood reading in her father's library or playing imaginative games with her brother Harry. Her writing was a natural extension of this, its immediacy and energy the product of "a life kept always young." *Elsie Piddock Skips in Her Sleep,* a particular favorite of the author and widely regarded as a miniature masterpiece, is taken from her second collection of stories, *Martin Pippin in the Daisy Field* (1937). In 1956 her achievements were acknowledged with both the Carnegie Medal and the Hans Christian Andersen Award. In her honor, a prize bearing her name is now awarded annually to mark an outstanding contribution to children's literature.

Charlotte Voake was singled out by Eleanor Farjeon's nephew, Gervase, as the ideal artist to interpret *Elsie Piddock Skips in Her Sleep*. Her illustrations display a natural exuberance and lightness of touch that characterize Farjeon's own work. Much admired as both an author and an illustrator, Charlotte Voake's other titles include *Ginger,* short-listed for the Kate Greenaway Medal and winner of a Nestlé Smarties Children's Book Prize Gold Medal; *Ginger Finds a Home;* and *Hello Twins,* a *New York Times Book Review* Best Illustrated Children's Book of the Year. Charlotte Voake lives in Surrey with her husband and two children.

First U.S. reformatted hardcover edition 2017

Library of Congress Catalog Card Number 96-26250
ISBN 978-0-7636-0790-6 (original hardcover)
ISBN 978-0-7636-3810-8 (paperback)
ISBN 978-0-7636-9055-7 (reformatted hardcover)

16 17 18 19 20 21 CCP 10 9 8 7 6 5 4 3 2 1

Printed in Shenzhen, Guangdong, China

This book was typeset in Stempel Schneidler.
The illustrations were done in watercolor and ink.

Candlewick Press
99 Dover Street
Somerville, Massachusetts 02144

visit us at www.candlewick.com